STAR WARS

OFFICIAL ANNUAL 2017

HOW TO BUILD CHOPPER AND EZRA

CONTENTS

MYSTERIOUS MASTER

A mighty Jedi Master stands before you. Find out who it is by circling the letters in the triangles that are the same colour as the Jedi's lightsaber blade. Then write the letters in the white boxes by matching them to the number in the centre of each triangle.

U
1
M
T
D
3
K
C
G
5
W
G
J
7
H
N
D
8
R
K
B
2
I
A
B
6
D
I
E
4
A
M
U
9
A
M
1 2 3 4 5 6 7 8 9

ENDLESS WAR

The Jedi forces have been in a constant struggle with the Sith Lords. Look at the battle between the two sides and mark the starship parts that can't be found in the scene.

1
2
3
4
5
6

HORNED WARRIOR

Qui-Gon Jinn must do everything in his power to defeat Darth Maul. Look at the small pictures below and mark the ones that are part of the menacing Sith warrior.

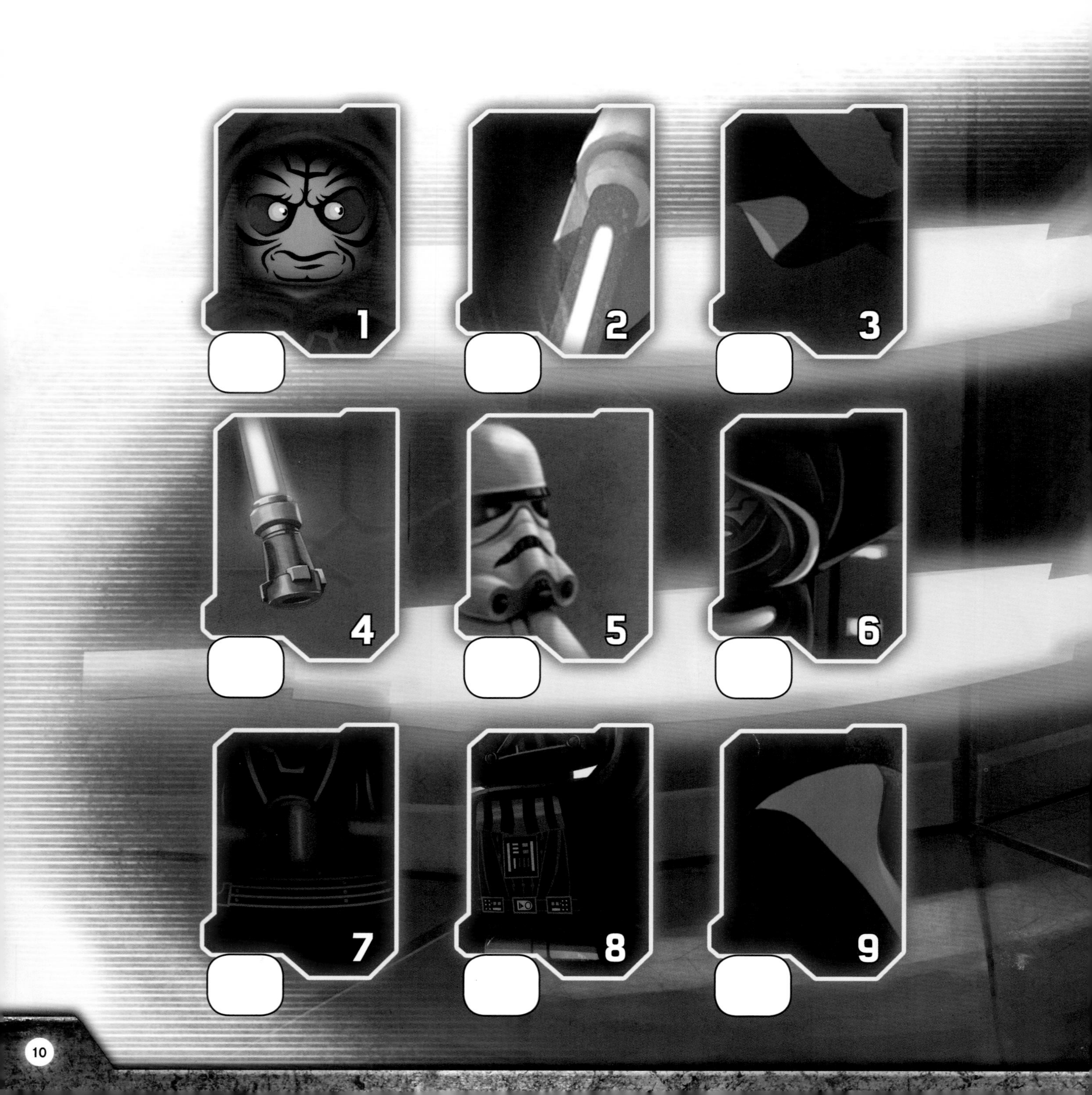

A MASTER'S WEAPON

Arm the Jedi with their lightsabers. The symbol next to each weapon is made up of two parts found near their Masters. Connect the parts to find out who owns each lightsaber.

QUI-GON JINN
YODA

FIXER-UPPER

ANAKIN SKYWALKER IS CONSTANTLY MESSING WITH THINGS!
YES, MASTER.

LAST TIME HE MOUNTED A JUICER ON R2-D2!

WHAT ABOUT THAT 'UPGRADE' HE MADE TO C-3PO? THAT DIDN'T END WELL EITHER, DID IT?

WHO PUTS ROLLER SKATES ON A PROTOCOL DROID, ANYWAY?

OBI-WAN, YOU HAVE TO KEEP AN EYE ON HIM. WHO KNOWS WHAT HE'LL COME UP WITH NEXT ...

A MOMENT LATER ...
HERE YOU GO, MASTER. I'VE MADE SOME IMPROVEMENTS TO YOUR LIGHTSABER.

WHAT DID YOU DO THIS TIME, ANAKIN?

NOTHING MUCH. I JUST TURNED IT INTO A TORCH!

FIELD MISSION

A group of Republic soldiers is looking for pieces of a wrecked Separatist starship on a weedy planet. Track it down by finding all the parts in the frames.

4 ×
4 ×
6 ×

JEDI POWER

Ezra, a young rebel from the planet Lothal, has discovered that he can use the Force. So far he can make these bricks float in any order he likes. Finish the repeating pattern he is making opposite by writing the right letters in the gaps.

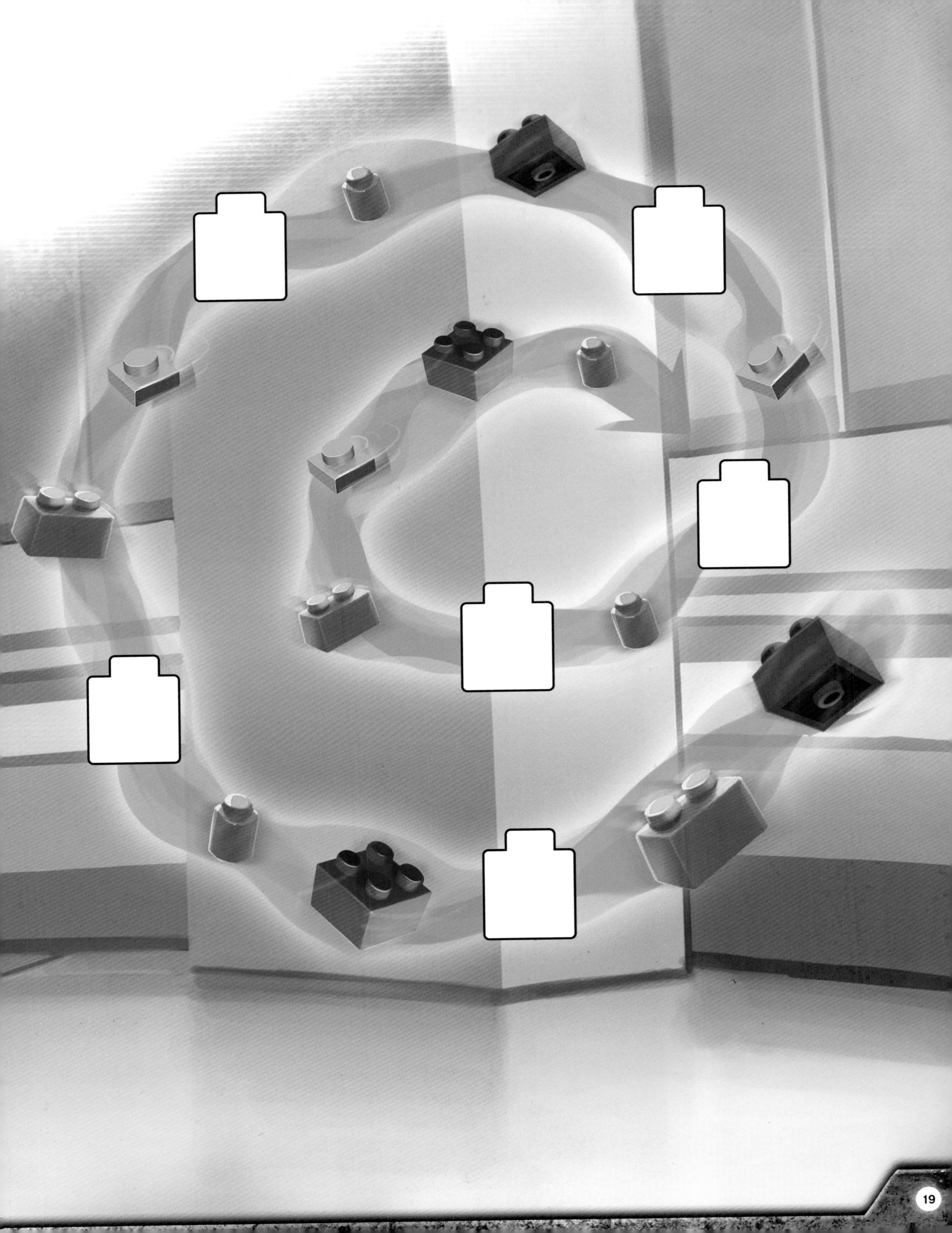

IMPERIAL BIRTHDAY

The corridors on the Death Star are very draughty. Help the Dark Lord cross the maze before the candle on his birthday cake goes out. Be quick, the Emperor can't wait to eat his tasty cake!

FINISH

START

ADJUTANT GUARD

You must place two guards on the opposite page at once! Draw lines to put each part of them in the right place. Darth Sidious loves how the red of the Royal Guards' capes matches his angry character.

1
2
3
4
5
6
7
8

SPACE MISTAKES

How perceptive are you? Find a character in each picture that doesn't match the other three, and circle them with a pen. Can you also spot a lightsaber hidden in each picture?

I SENSE SOMEONE'S HAVING VERY DARK THOUGHTS!
WHY DON'T I HAVE A JETPACK? IT'S OUTRAGEOUS! CAN SOMEONE DRAW ME ONE?

DARTH BUNGLER

While he was practising a new Force Push technique, Lord Vader scattered bricks all over the Death Star. Can you count all the flying bricks and write the numbers in the octagons before the stormtroopers clean them all up?

COSMIC FLIGHT

Only one of these devices will give Luke the correct location of his starship in relation to the planet he's flying by. Which one is it?

1

4

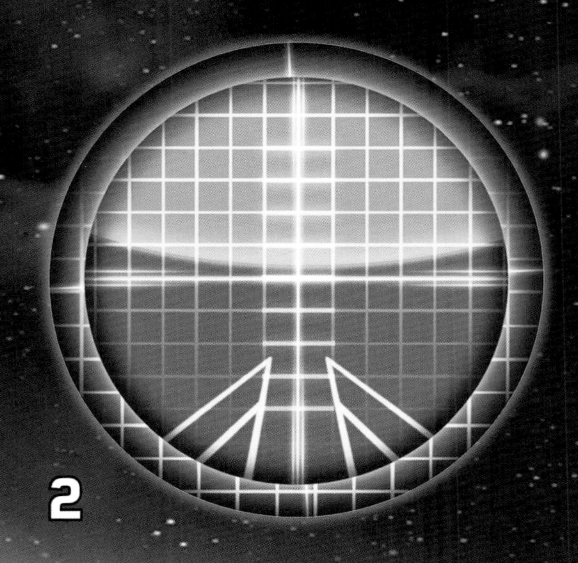
2

5

3

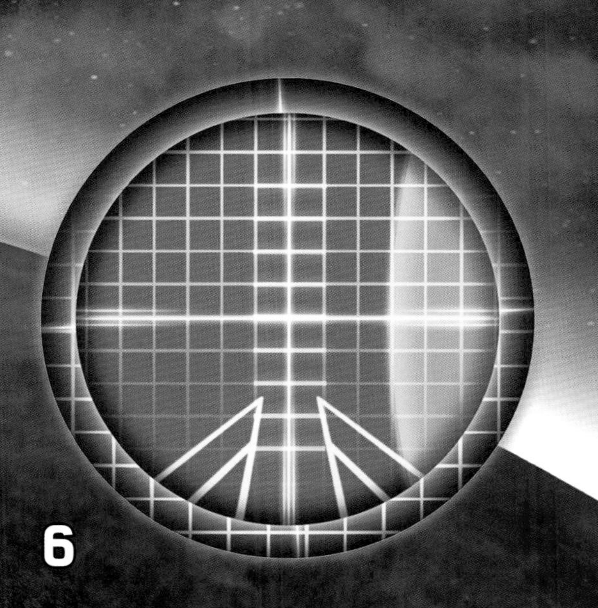
6

SERVANTS OF THE DARK SIDE

Darth Sidious can always rely on his evil allies to be ready to defend his Empire. Connect all the dark side collaborators to their descriptions.

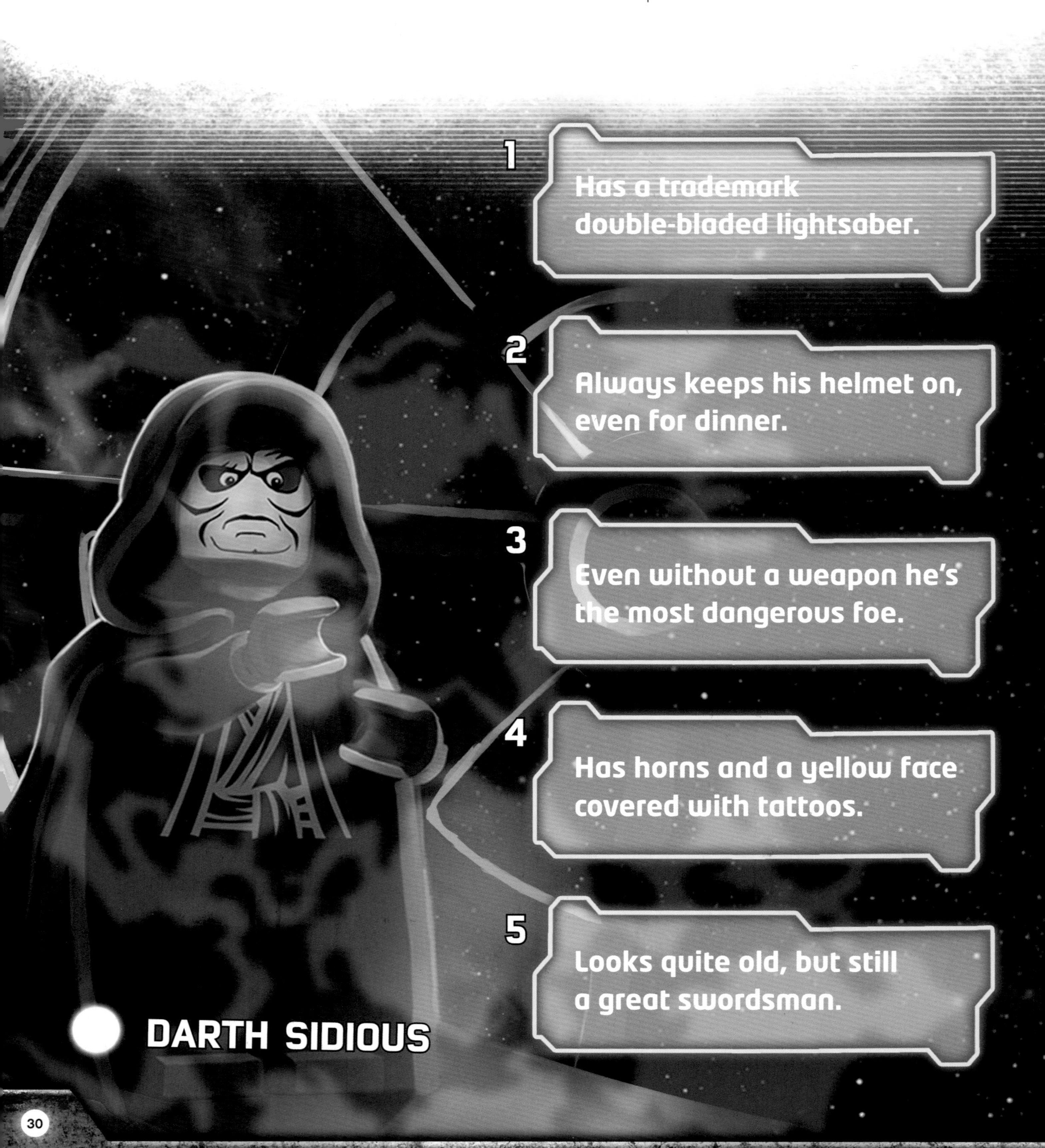

DARTH VADER

SAVAGE OPRESS

COUNT DOOKU

DARTH MAUL

SUBSPACE CHASE

A whole TIE fighter squadron is chasing the *Millennium Falcon!* But two fighters lost some parts on the flight and have to return to base. Find the two fighters that are different from the others.

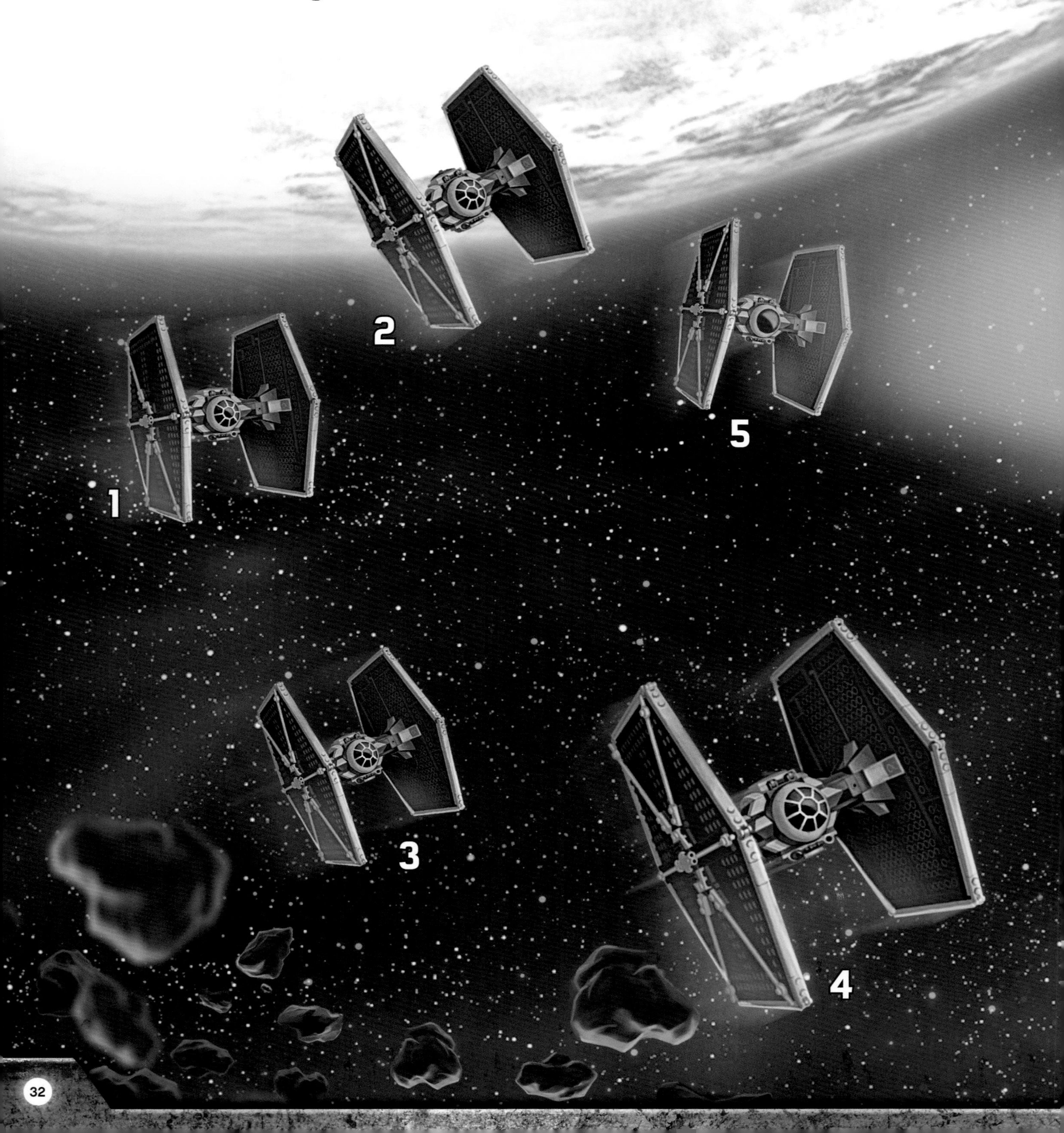

SHOCKING SNEEZE

Darth Sidious never accidentally zaps anyone with Force lightning – except for when he sneezes! Discover why his subordinates never stick around to say 'bless you' by finding where each piece of the picture should go.

A
D
B
E
C
F

IMPORTANT COUNCIL

The rebels know exactly where to attack the Death Star. Can you find its weak spot? It is encoded in the part of the hologram that has the same six symbols as shown in the frame below.

REBEL DANCE-OFF

Even a rebel celebrating the Death Star's destruction isn't allowed to dance in the same row or column twice. Knowing this, complete the empty spaces on the dance floor grid by writing in the correct numbers. Then count the onlookers in the background enjoying the dance-off and write their number in the octagon.

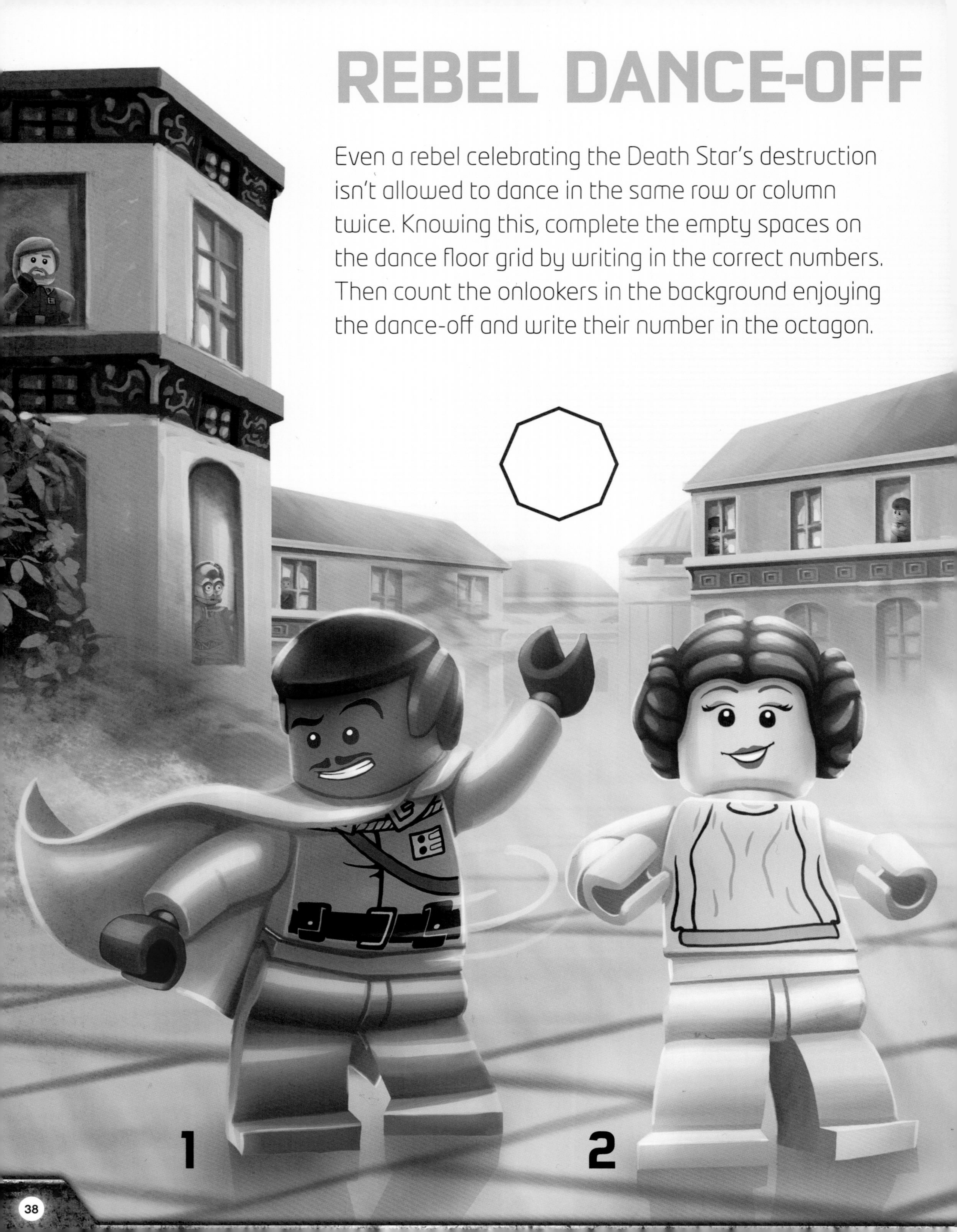

3
4

FOOOOOD!

This big, hairy monster is very hungry. One piece of spaghetti will lead him to a bowl full of tasty food. Show Chewie which one it is.

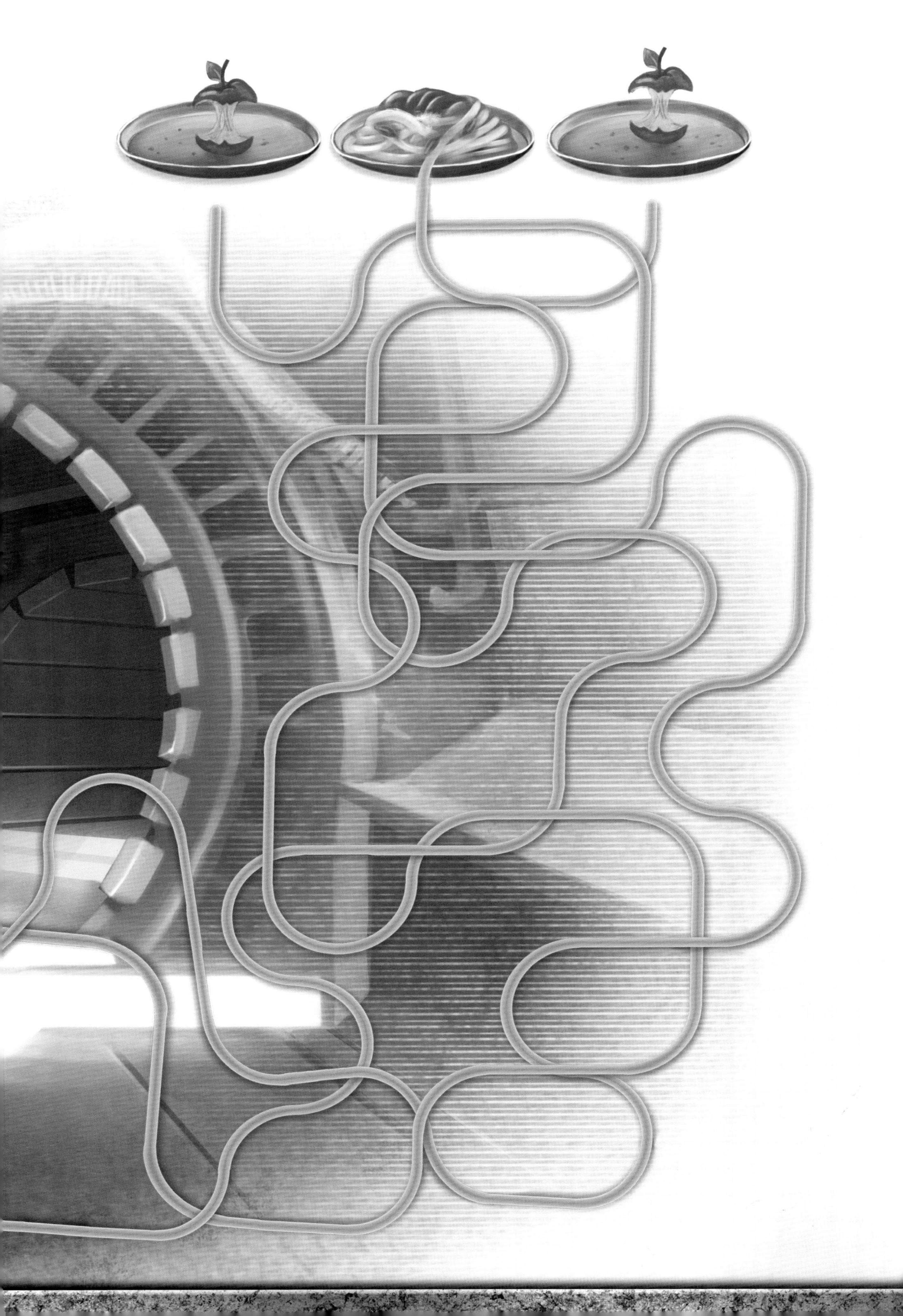

THE REBEL ATTACK!

These small rebel starships are attacking the Imperial convoy! Look carefully at the small pictures below and tick four that match the scene.

MAINTENANCE DAY

There comes a time in every droid's life when general maintenance is needed. Look at the picture and circle which of these statements are true and which are false.

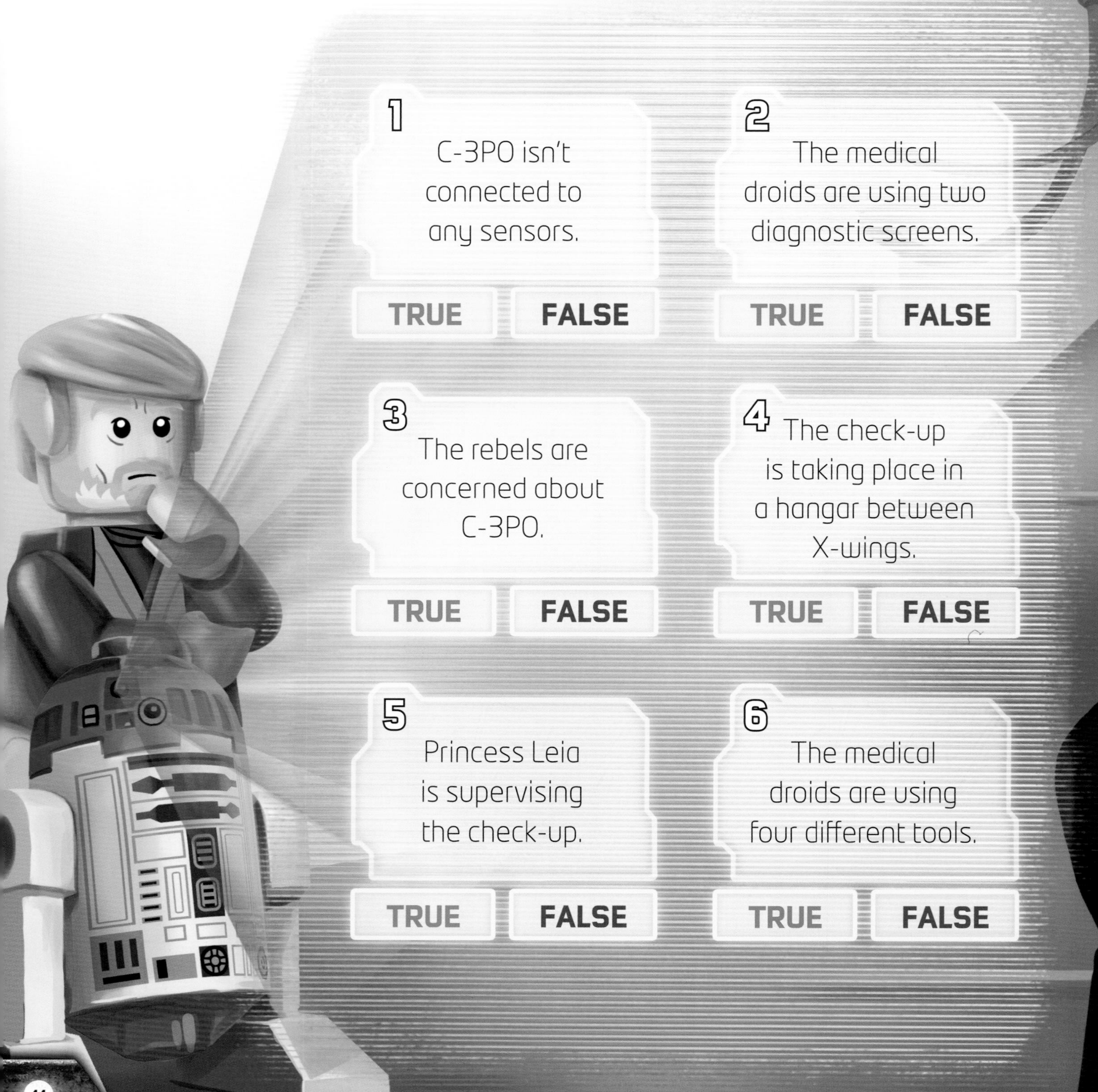

1 C-3PO isn't connected to any sensors.

TRUE FALSE

2 The medical droids are using two diagnostic screens.

TRUE FALSE

3 The rebels are concerned about C-3PO.

TRUE FALSE

4 The check-up is taking place in a hangar between X-wings.

TRUE FALSE

5 Princess Leia is supervising the check-up.

TRUE FALSE

6 The medical droids are using four different tools.

TRUE FALSE

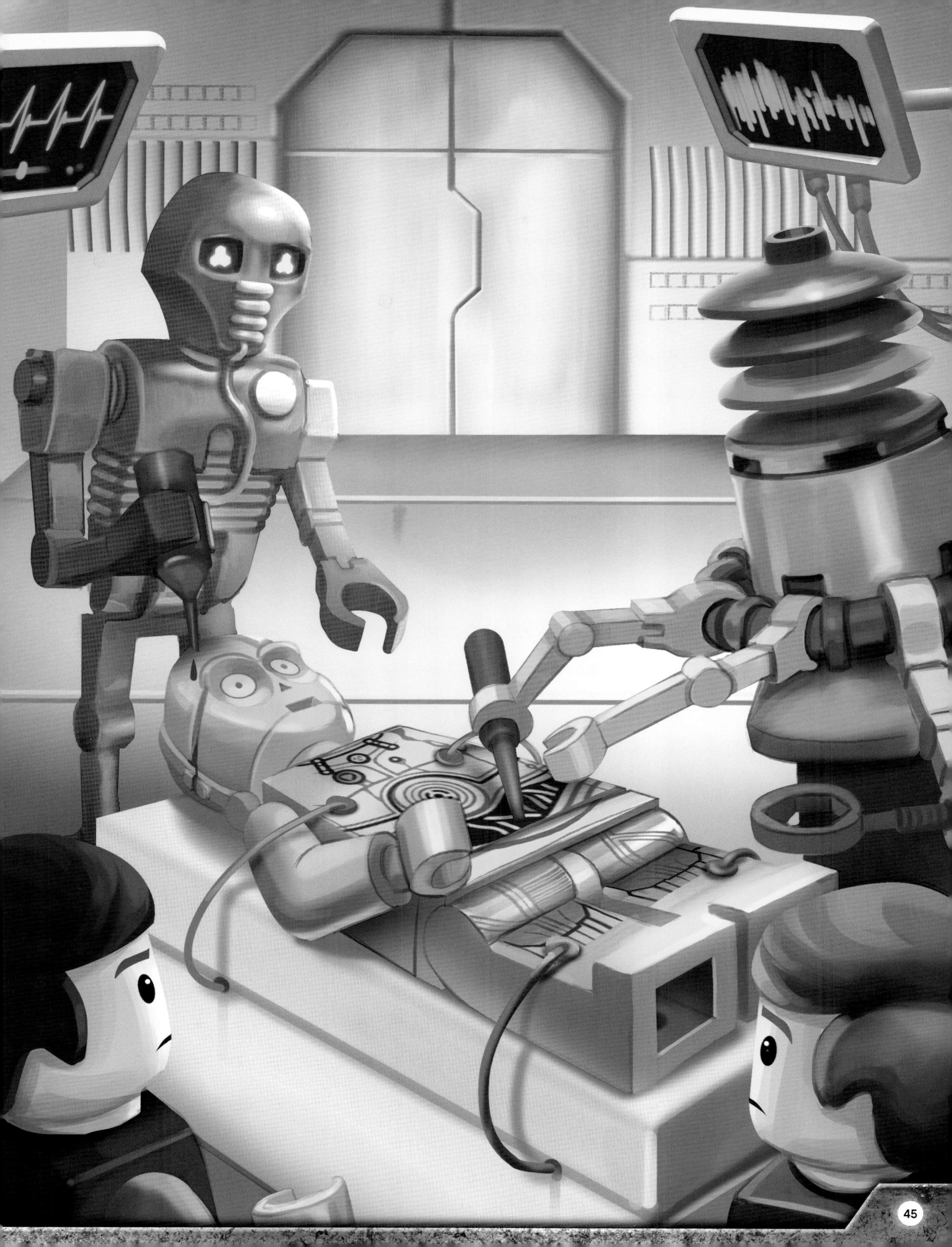

DROID AGENTS

Admiral Ackbar has a mission for the bravest droids in the galaxy. C-3PO is ready to go! Get R2-D2 ready by colouring him in to make him difficult to see at night.

HOLOCONFERENCE

No one knows what secrets Darth Vader and the Emperor tell each other. Can you find four differences between the pictures of the gossipy Emperor?

1
2
3
4

ROBO-BARBER

I THINK IT'S TIME TO GIVE CHEWIE A HAIRCUT.
YEAH, HE'S REALLY LET HIMSELF GO THIS TIME.

BUT WE DON'T HAVE ANY SCISSORS ON BOARD. ANY IDEAS?

ARTOO-DETOO WILL DO IT!

GOOD JOB, ARTOO!
BUT I'D RUN NOW IF I WERE YOU!

FROM JEDI TO SITH

C-3PO is reading a story about Anakin Skywalker to the rebels. Put the pictures of the tale in the right order by numbering them from 1-4. Start from the early days of the ex-Jedi, and finish with him becoming a Sith! How many Ewoks are hiding in the forest? Write their number in the box.

DESERT SCAVENGE

Rey is in the Jakku desert. Help her sift through all the scrap and salvage the old droids and starship parts from the sand. Label all the starship parts with a '1' and the old droids with a '2'. Then add up how many there are of each and write the numbers in the boxes. Which does she find more of?

SHIP PARTS
OLD DROIDS

X-WING SQUAD LEADER

The X-wing squadron is practising battle formations before an important mission. Shoot all the targets by crossing out the letters pointed at by arrows. Reading from left to right and top to bottom, the ones left will give you the name of the squad leader. Write their name in the boxes below.

I P L W G O H
B Z E P M R D
A W J Y A O S
M F C R S P E
U B D R C O M
Z J E N P A G

ANSWERS

Pg. 6–7
MYSTERIOUS MASTER

MACE WINDU

Pg. 8–9
ENDLESS WAR

Pg. 10–11
HORNED WARRIOR

2

6

9

Pg. 12–13
A MASTER'S WEAPON

KIT FISTO

MACE WINDU

YODA

QUI-GON JINN

Pg. 16–17
FIELD MISSION

Pg. 18–19
JEDI POWER

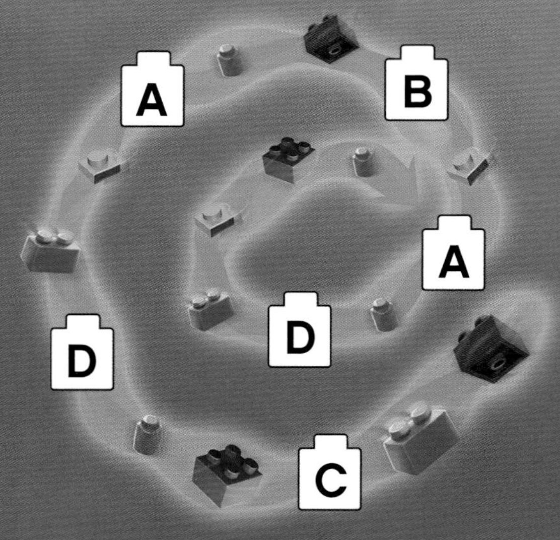

Pg. 20–21
IMPERIAL BIRTHDAY

FINISH

START

Pg. 22–23
ADJUTANT GUARD

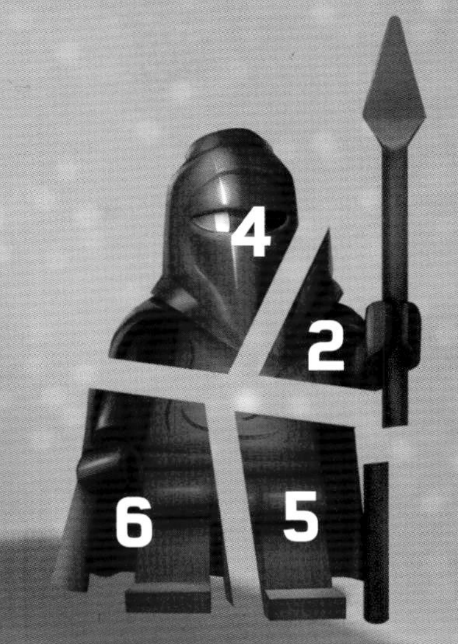

Pg. 24–25
SPACE MISTAKES

Pg. 26–27
DARTH BUNGLER

6 4 7 5 4

Pg. 28–29
COSMIC FLIGHT

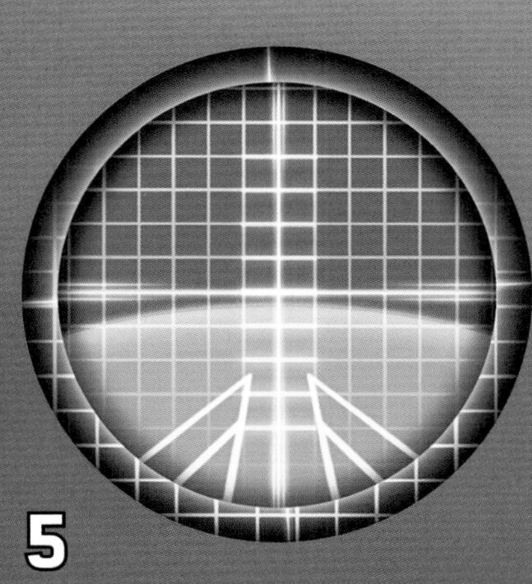

5

Pg. 30–31
SERVANTS OF THE DARK SIDE

DARTH MAUL 1
DARTH VADER 2
DARTH SIDIOUS 3
SAVAGE OPRESS 4
COUNT DOOKU 5

Pg. 32–33
SUBSPACE CHASE

1

5

Pg. 34–35
SHOCKING SNEEZE

Pg. 36–37
IMPORTANT COUNCIL

Pg. 38–39
REBEL DANCE-OFF

ON-LOOKERS: 5

Pg. 40–41
FOOOOOD!

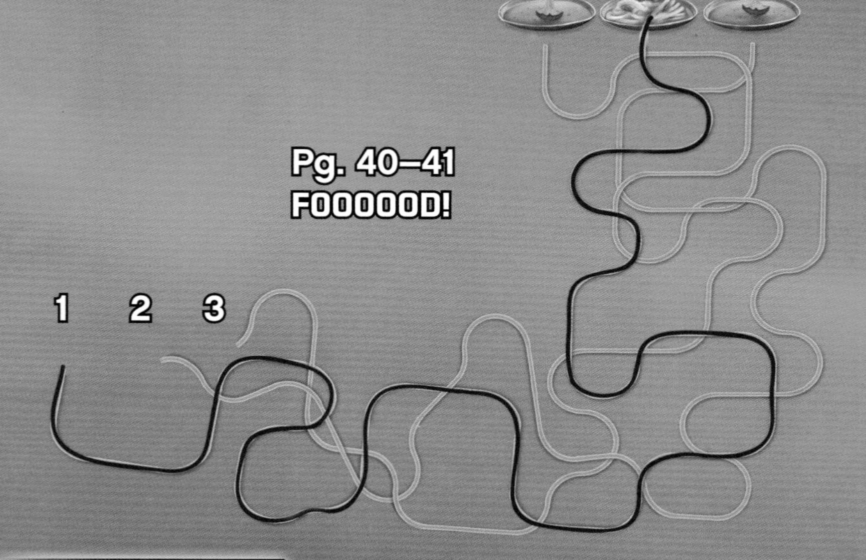

Pg. 42–43
THE REBEL ATTACK!

Pg. 44–45
MAINTENANCE DAY

1 – FALSE
2 – TRUE
3 – TRUE
4 – FALSE
5 – FALSE
6 – FALSE

Pg. 48–49
HOLOCONFERENCE

Pg. 52–53
FROM JEDI TO SITH

EWOKS: 5

Pg. 54–55
DESERT SCAVENGE

Pg. 56–57
X-WING SQUAD LEADER

POE DAMERON

THERE ARE MORE SHIP PARTS.

16

9

1 – SHIP PARTS

2 – OLD DROIDS